This book belongs to

John Morse

Petz™ Series

Chili Dogs

Carla Tedrow

FamilyVision Press
New York

FamilyVision Press™
For The Family That Reads Together™
An imprint of Multi Media Communicators, Inc.
575 Madison Avenue, Suite 1006
New York, NY 10022

FamilyVision Press™, Petz™, Chili Dogs™ and For The Family That Reads Together™ are registered trademarks of Multi Media Communicators, Inc.

Illustrator, Lou Grant
Typesetter, Samuel Chapin

Library of Congress Catalog Card Number: 93-071559

ISBN 1-56969-325-0

10 9 8 7 6 5 4 3 2 1
First Edition

Printed in the United States of America

To my husband, Tom,
and my children, C.T., Tyler and Tara,
who enrich my life every day.

A Message to Parents and Guardians from FamilyVision Press

At FamilyVision, we believe that families should read together. Whether your children set aside a specially reserved family reading time or whether they read books, newspapers, trading cards, or cereal boxes at the breakfast table, please urge your children to read, read, read!

So where do you start? At your children's earliest age and throughout their lifetime, read and discuss books aloud during regularly scheduled reading times. Make reading time a special time—take turns reading, encourage discussion and questions, have grandparents relate personal stories from their childhood, ask your child to retell parts of the story and anticipate what will happen next.

Let them hear the music and power of the written word spoken aloud. Enhance the storytelling moment by varying facial expressions, tone, and pace as you read. Give the reluctant reader flexibility to move around or use crayons and pencils while the story is being read. And, for younger children, add another dimension to reading with a "read and play" experience. For example, when reading our Petz Series, let your child hold a stuffed animal. When reading is completed, help your child play out the storyline or create new adventures.

Where can you get your books? Make the local bookstore and library part of your family's regular routine. Take them to the library's storytime and watch for such special events as readings and personal appearances at bookstores. Remember to take a book everywhere! It's amazing when and where there will be time to read.

When you read with your children, they will learn firsthand that a book can be a wonderful thing. It can be a vehicle for traveling to new worlds, a key to unlocking the imagination, and a wonderful opportunity for sharing special moments with your children.

Chili Dogs

Taco and Tamale, two friendly Dalmatians, lived with their owners in San Antonio, Texas. José and María Cabreras loved spending a lot of time with Taco and Tamale.

José and María had to work long hours at their open-air restaurant, a *cantina* in La Villita, the oldest part of the city. They enjoyed bringing Taco and Tamale with them.

Their landlord, Mr. Derrick, was a selfish man. He wanted to close down their restaurant so he could turn it into a parking lot. He thought he would make more money that way. The Cabreras family would have to go!

José and María were afraid of him. Taco and Tamale were afraid of him. Even Mr. Derrick's own dogs were afraid of him. He was not a nice man.

Mr. Derrick's Dalmatian dogs were not happy and carefree like Taco and Tamale. They were raised only for shows and to make money.

He liked using his dogs to win money and be the center of attention. What he didn't like was caring for them or feeding them.

People around town talked about how poorly Mr. Derrick treated his dogs.
He kept them locked in small cages without room to play.

He would yell at the dogs, "No food for you until show time!"

Taco and Tamale would sneak behind the bushes and think about helping their friends. "Some day," Tamale would say, "we will free them."

When the Cabreras were unable to pay their rent Mr. Derrick was happy. If they did not pay his rent he would have them evicted...thrown out! And he would try to keep all their possessions—including Taco and Tamale! Imagine, he thought, the restaurant and the dogs too.

Mr. Derrick told José he had thirty days to find the money or else.

José said, "You may get the restaurant, but the Taco and Tamale? Never!"

Mr. Derrick just smirked and said, "We'll see."

The Dalmatians were scared. They loved their family and wanted to keep the restaurant. They decided to work just as hard as José and María.

They all worked together. José prepared yummy tacos for the children and chili enchiladas for the adults. María seated customers and waited on tables. Taco and Tamale would wander the open air tables entertaining the customers with tricks.

Everyone began to know how the Dalmatians loved hot, spicy, Mexican food. Soon customers would give their leftovers to Taco and Tamale. In return, the two dogs would do even more tricks.

As more and more customers came, José and María were close to raising the rent money. But close would not be good enough for Mr. Derrick.

Suddenly, when everything looked darkest, some bright possibilities appeared.

Tamale was going to have puppies and soon there would be a Dalmatian puppy contest!

Now everyone was excited. Tamale would soon be having puppies and José would enter them into the contest—for a prize of fifty thousand dollars.

"This is the happiest news we could hear," said María. "If Tamale's puppies win we can pay Mr. Derrick and buy the restaurant!"

Mr. Derrick heard about the puppies and the contest. Now he was determined to have the *cantina* and the dogs, and said, "You have only a few days left to get me my money. Soon everything you own will be mine!"

José ordered Mr. Derrick off the property. Taco nipped and yipped at him as he left.

Mr. Derrick came up with a plan to close them down. He would chase away their customers, scare the suppliers, and shut down the place once and for all.

Then María and José would have to leave. If all else failed, he would flood the restaurant.

Meanwhile, no one knew of his plan. José and María were worried about Tamale and her strange cravings.

Taco worried too.

Tamale wanted to eat nothing but chili! She ate chili for breakfast, chili for lunch and chili for dinner! She just ate, and ate, and ate! They were so busy watching Tamale that they didn't see Mr. Derrick's plans taking place. Fewer customers, fewer deliveries, fewer dollars.

One day Mr. Derrick walked by the restaurant and put CLOSED signs on the door. The people in the neighborhood saw the lights on and went inside anyway. This made Mr. Derrick angry.

Next, Mr. Derrick stood in the alley and sent away all the deliverymen. That night María and José could not open because they did not have enough ingredients to make the food.

Finally, Mr. Derrick decided to flood the restaurant. He sneaked into the restaurant one night and opened all the faucets! What a mess! The firemen had to come to pump out all the water. Everything was ruined!

The next morning, José and María realized they were out of business. "What are we to do? We have no money and no restaurant. We can't pay Mr. Derrick."

When the Cabreras returned home they had one piece of good news: Tamale was ready to have her babies. It was their only hope. José and María kept their fingers crossed that they would have a show winner. "I hope one of the puppies will win the prize," José exclaimed.

When six puppies arrived, Taco took one look and rolled on his back!

Tamale's pups were red and white! Instead of black Dalmatian spots the puppies were covered with red chili-pepper shaped spots!

"We are sure to win the Puppy Contest!" Maria said.

José looked at the pups and laughed. "Tamale ate too much chili!" Then he remembered the puppy contest and told María, "It doesn't say anything about what color spots the Dalmatians have to have."

María asked, "How will we describe them?"

José looked at the six puppies with red chili spots and shouted, "Why, we'll call them Chili Dogs—the rarest pups in the world!"

When word of the amazing Chili Dogs reached the media, reporters came from all over. The puppies appeared on television and in newspapers everywhere. They were famous.

Only one person was not happy about the puppies—Mr. Derrick! He wanted them for his own.

He thought to himself, "I must have them! I will keep that family from winning the $50,000 dog show. I'll have the restaurant and those Chili Dogs."

Tamale was a sweet mother to her puppies. She kept them well fed and clean.

Taco was the proud father of six red-and-white Dalmatian puppies that were the talk of the town!

The day of the puppy contest drew near. José and María decided to paint their white van with red chili peppers!

What a fun way to drive Taco, Tamale, and the Chili Dogs to the contest!

In the meantime, Mr. Derrick was busy thinking of a way to keep the Cabreras family from making it to the contest. He did everything from placing nails on the street...

...to setting up fake roadblocks.

Finally the big day arrived. José and María were so excited about the contest they almost forgot to put the puppies in the van!

María said, "If we win the contest our troubles will be over!"

José nodded. "We have to win. It is our only hope of keeping the restaurant and opening again."

Taco and Tamale kept their paws crossed that their little Chili Dogs would save the day.

When the Cabreras family reached the end of their street they heard loud popping noises and felt a thud.

All four tires had gone flat!

"Oh, no!" José gasped. "Now we will be late for the contest!"

María calmed José down. "We will work as a team and repair the tires," she said.

"But we have only one spare tire." José frowned.

"Then we will have to find another way to fix the other three," María said.

As María and José hurried to fix the flat tires, Mr. Derrick was hiding behind the bushes, smirking. "That should delay them for a while. They only have one spare so they'll never make it to the show. My plan is working!" he laughed.

A man who owned a tire store pulled up in his truck. "Do you need some help?" he asked. "I have some spare tires in the back of my truck."

"You are the answer to our prayers!" José said.

Everyone was thrilled. Taco, Tamale, and the Chili Dogs wagged their tails in excitement.

Before long, the van was ready to go. José and María thanked the truck driver as he drove off. "Don't forget to stop by the restaurant for a free dinner!"

Mr. Derrick fumed as he watched the van of happy people and dogs drive off. "They will never get past my next trap," he chuckled.

Sure enough, the roadblock confused José and María. Mr. Derrick's fake detour would take them miles out of their way and they would miss the contest. When José stopped the van to consult a map, Taco decided to investigate.

Taco whispered to Tamale, "Stay with the pups. I'm going to check things out." With a powerful leap Taco jumped down from the van.

"Please be careful," Tamale pleaded.

Mr. Derrick, following behind, saw Taco leave the pups unguarded and thought this would be his chance to snatch them.

While José and María looked at their map, Mr. Derrick crept up to the open door of the van.

Tamale was surprised to find Mr. Derrick reaching for the puppies.

Taco sensed something was wrong and turned to head back to the van.

Mr. Derrick heard Taco before seeing him. A growl filled the air. Taco jumped on Mr. Derrick and took a firm hold of his shirt from the back, pulling him away from his family.

José and María heard the commotion and rushed to the back of the van.
There they found Mr. Derrick struggling with Taco. "What are you doing?"
María asked Mr. Derrick before he escaped from Taco and ran off.

José and María congratulated Taco for being such a brave dog. Tamale was so worried that Mr. Derrick would try something else that she and the puppies rode in the front seat all the way to the show.

When they arrived at the contest, Taco, Tamale, and their owners were relieved. They were in time. "We finally made it," María said.

From the moment they carried the basket of Chili Dogs into the hall, they were a hit.

It was not hard for the judges to decide who should win the $50,000.
Mr. Derrick stood fuming while the Chili Dogs received their ribbons.

Though they were happy to win, Taco and Tamale felt sad for Mr. Derrick's dogs, locked up in small cages.

Tamale decided to take matters into her own paws.

Tamale quietly asked the Dalmatians if they wanted to be free from Mr. Derrick.

"Oh, yes!" they all barked excitedly.

"If you're ready to try a better life, then on the count of three, I'll open your cages. Then you can chase Mr. Derrick away."

The dogs burst from their cages and leapt at Mr. Derrick. He turned and ran from the hall as all the dogs barked and yipped their disapproval of him.

No one helped Mr. Derrick since everyone knew how mean he'd been to his dogs.

Mr. Derrick now understood he could not mistreat animals.

José and María decided to use the contest money won by the amazing Chili Dogs for two important things.

They would buy the restaurant from Mr. Derrick so that it would always be a *cantina* and never a parking lot. José set to work fixing up the kitchen and drying the place out. He repainted the outside in a very special way.

And they would buy a new house. It would be a home for José and María as well as Taco and Tamale and the Chili Dogs. And it would be a home for Mr. Derrick's Dalmatians as well.

Now José and María owned the restaurant and it was busier than ever.

Tourists from all over came to San Antonio to see the amazing Chili Dogs of Amigo's Mexican Restaurant.

About the Author...

CARLA K. TEDROW is an actress, author and book editor who manages to juggle her career with raising three young children in Florida. Born in Cape Girardeau, Missouri, Carla brings the values of her small town upbringing into her children's books, always striving to inspire and entertain.

Carla said, "Having read hundreds of books to my children over the years, I've developed a keen insight into what children want to hear and read. In each of my books I strive to capture their imagination, tickle their funnybones and leave them with a message."